I WANT IT NOW!

Helping Children Deal With Disappointment and Frustration

By
Chris Loftis

Illustrations by
Darryl Moore

New Horizon Press
Far Hills, New Jersey

Loftis, Chris
I Want it Now!: Helping Children Deal With Disappointment and Frustration

Illustrations: Darryl Moore
Cover Design: Norma Erler Rahn
Interior Design: Susan M. Sanderson

Library of Congress Control Number: 2003100286

ISBN: 0-88282-237-3
SMALL HORIZONS
A Division of New Horizon Press

2007   2006   2005   2004   2003/   5   4   3   2   1

Printed in Hong Kong

There it was,
all shiny and new.
It had big rubber tires;
its color was blue.

It could climb any mountain.
It could race down any street.
It could go as far as the eye can see
and moved much faster than your feet.

Billy had finally found
a longtime dream come true
on page 206 of a catalog
between tables and shampoo.

He knew that very instant
that the bike should be his own.
He was going to convince his parents
to order his gift by telephone.

Billy was going to tell them
to pick up the phone and call right away
to buy the bike, that awsome bike
and really make his day.

This would be the birthday present
that Billy had been wishing for so long.
Just thinking about getting the gift
made him burst into joyous song.

The 62-Z-4 Stingray
could make him happier than ever before.
He thought about the bike a moment
and decided he would never want anything more.

When Billy told this to his parents,
he expected that they would smile,
but they looked at the price
and looked at each other and thought for quite a while.

Then from their mouths
came words Billy hoped he would not hear
and from his eye and down his cheek
rolled a giant, shiny tear.

His parents sighed,
their faces downcast.
They looked at him sadly,
and said very fast,

"We are so sorry, honey,
but please, understand
this wonderful gift
just cannot be planned."

Mom said, "Dad lost his job, Son,
and though I am working two,
we just do not have the money
to buy this bike for you."

"But please, the bike is perfect.
It is really all I need.
I am a good boy,
and I deserve this good deed.

"I clean up my toys.
I do well in school.
I feed the cocker spaniel.
I never break a rule.

"I clean my plate at dinner.
I come home when I'm told.
I shoveled the snow last winter
and boy, was it cold!"

"I… I…," Billy stuttered,
he could not make the words come.
He looked over at his parents
and saw that they were both quite glum.

"You are a great son, Billy,
about that you are right.
We are very, very sorry,
right now our money is tight.

"I'll tell you what, "
Billy's mom said with cheer.
"I'll make your favorite treat,
an ice cream float with root beer."

"I do not want a float;
I want the blue bike!
I want nothing else;
there is nothing else I would like.

"That blue bike is my dream,
as I told you before.
It is just what I want,
nothing less, nothing more.

"You think I will forget,
but that just is not true.
So, Mom and Dad,
what are you going to do?"

With that Billy ran down the hall to his room,
slammed the door and began crying.
His parents were sad and stared down at the floor,
both of them feeling sorry and each of them sighing.

Their little boy was crying.
Their son was feeling blue.
Inside, they cried as well,
for they felt badly too.

Oh, not just about the bicycle,
but because Billy's dreams would not come true…
You see, the people who really love you
share each of your dreams, be they many or few…

Now Billy and his parents
were all quite upset,
but not with each other.
They had begun to forget…

…that sometimes hopes are hopeless
and not all dreams come true.
Often life seems crazy
and there is nothing you can do.

It is like a promise somehow broken,
a rainbow hidden by a cloud,
a wonderful friendship that has been lost,
a deed of which you are not proud.

Billy's parents knew very well
just how their boy was feeling,
for they both had their own lost dreams
with which they were dealing.

You see, we all have dreams,
some big and some small.
They are each and every one important,
to each and to all.

Not all dreams can come true.
Some dreams must be changed…
some have to be gussied up
and others rearranged.

Some have to be given up
and some left behind
or at least put on hold, so
a new dream you can find.

That night the family lay in bed,
struggling with defeat.
Not one of them slept well,
each one felt the heat.

Then a breeze swept through Billy's window,
a welcome gift indeed,
it cooled him then did something else
to help with Billy's need.

The wind blew the catalog,
which flipped to a brand new page.
The boy jumped up and saw on it
a treasure for any age.

There, on page 283,
a family in a park,
a boy and his parents,
playing ball until dark.

As he stared at the happy family
smiling and laughing with one another,
he felt this was better than any old bike;
his family was a gift like no other.

And that's when he realized
that just what he wanted, he already had.
Billy knew when he told his parents,
they would not feel so bad.

So Billy burst into his parents' room
and jumped on the bed where they lay.
He kissed each one and pointed to the page,
and in a jubilant voice he did happily say:

"Check out this picture!
Forget about that bike!
A fun day with you two
is what I would like."

"I think that would be
the best birthday gift.
It would give all our hearts
a much needed lift.

"I think it would be a much better gift;
we'll all be happy, I promise, you'll see.
Mom, Dad, it will give us our smiles back,
that is what is most important to me".

Then his parents looked down at the eyes
of the boy who had so badly wanted a bike
and saw a kinder, just as happy,
truly wonderful young tyke.

That is when it all happened.
That is when they knew.
They decided at that moment
to make Billy's dream come true.

This new dream of togetherness
was one they could give from inside,
as it could be freely offered
if they stood by each other's side.

Dad said, "Okay, son.
The answer is YES.
But there are some issues
we need to address."

"Anything," Billy blurted out.
"I will do whatever it will take."
"Well, good," his parents said together,
"that is a deal we can make."

"In addition to spending the day together,
we also will start to save money for you.
Then the bike you want so much will be yours.
With patience, both dreams can come true.

"You will need to help us save the money
and your dream will become a goal.
We can work together as a family.
We can each play a helpful role."

"Wow, spending time together and a bike too?"
Billy said happily, "Thank you, Mom and Dad!
You are great people and I love you both.
This will be the best birthday I ever have had."

Billy's mom said, "So it is settled.
We will put money in a jar.
We will all work together
and soon our savings will go far.

"We are all very excited,
because your birthday is just two weeks away.
I will stay home from work;
we will celebrate as a family that day."

As birthdays always do,
soon enough Billy's came.
Finally, his heart's desire
he was able to claim.

The family went to a nearby park,
where they played for many hours
among the trees and fields of green
and brightly colored flowers.

It was good to laugh
and good to jump
even though Billy got
some bruises and a bump.

Dreams can also be like that;
just to make them come true,
you must endure the bumps and bruises
and even a scrape or two.

Billy's dream was not the only one
transformed that happy day.
His parents discovered they could learn
to see life in a whole new way.

They learned the most important thing
that they could give their son,
was not a bike or fancy clothes
or things that cost a ton.

Instead they had to give him
the ability to stand tall,
to wish, to hope and to dream,
to be fair but most of all…

To accomplish, to achieve,
to be bold and be kind,
to be brave and to be just,
with a strong heart and mind.

To know what is true
and to see what is fake,
what makes the heart full
and what makes it ache.

Just like Billy's bumps and scrapes,
His family learned that it is true
that along the path of life,
there will be some tough spots, too.

Indeed the most important thing to have
is the love that families share.
For the rough times will be made much easier
when you are with the people who care.

— The End —